THE DEPARTMENT
STORE GHOST

THE DEPARTMENT
STORE GHOST

THE DEPARTMENT STORE GHOST

by Bill and Rosalie Brown

Illustrated by Leonard Shortall

Xerox Education Publications

XEROX

Other Books by Bill and Rosalie Brown

THE FOREST FIREMEN

WHISTLE PUNK

THE BOY WHO GOT MAILED

BIG RIG

GIANT BIRTHDAY SALE
100 YEARS OLD TODAY

Grandpa Follet was mad clear through. First he was mad because he was a ghost, and the crowds on the sidewalk couldn't see him or feel him or hear him. Folks walked right *through* Grandpa.

He was mad, too, about his store. He had started it a hundred years ago and now he'd come back after all this time to find the store like *this!*

Grandpa Follet stood on the sidewalk in

front of the Follet Department Store and looked up at the new sign hung above the entrance. It read:

GIANT BIRTHDAY SALE
100 Years Old Today

The sign was decorated by a pink cardboard birthday cake. At one end of the sign Grandpa saw his own picture. He was dressed as he always was in his frock coat and top hat.

At the other end of the sign was a picture of his grandson, Bennett Follet. He had a round face, a bald head and a big friendly smile. He was the owner of the store now.

When Grandpa started the Follet Department Store it was just a little brick building one floor high. Now, a hundred years later, it was nine floors high and covered half a city block.

Grandpa looked in the window for the things he used to sell: saddles and bridles, tin washboards and washtubs and long winter underwear. Instead he saw things he'd never seen before: television sets and radios and toy rocket ships.

Grandpa looked up at his grandson's picture.

"Idiot!" he said. "What have you done to my store!"

Grandpa heard a bugle call ring out loud and clear. It came from inside the store. The crowds on the sidewalk pressed up against the big glass front doors. Grandpa knew the store was about to open.

First Grandpa saw thousands of lights come on, all at once, until the inside of the store was as bright as sunlight. Then he saw all of the staircases on the first floor start to move, some of them up and some of them down. Then the big glass front doors opened up all by themselves without anyone touching them.

Grandpa watched the crowds rush in, and the Giant Birthday Sale was on.

Grandpa saw the floorwalkers on the other
side of the big front doors. They were all
dressed up in dark blue suits with carnations
in their buttonholes. They smiled as the people
came in.

Grandpa saw salespeople standing at their counters, behind piles of towels or jewelry or glassware.

But Grandpa couldn't see anyone that looked like Bennett Follet.

"Why isn't my grandson in there running the store!" Grandpa muttered.

What he didn't know was that his grandson *was* running the store, even if Grandpa couldn't see Bennett.

If there was anything Bennett Follet liked better than Giant Birthday Sales, it was push buttons, and he'd had the Follet Department Store rigged up so he could push buttons right in his office and run almost everything.

Bennett's office was on the balcony of the store. Through the window he could see everything that happened on the main floor below. Beside the window was a push-button panel with rows and rows of buttons and rows and rows of tiny lights. Bennett could push a button and every light in the store would come on. He could push another button and the escalators would start to move. He could push a button that opened the glass front doors.

Bennett looked down at the crowds coming up to the counters to buy things.

"Wouldn't Grandpa be happy and proud if he could see this!" Bennett said. "And wouldn't he just love running a store with push buttons!"

Bennett pushed one more button. A phonograph record began to play "Happy Birthday to You."

Out in front, Grandpa heard the sound booming from loudspeakers inside the store. He looked again at the crowds in there, at the moving stairways and the doors that opened by themselves.

"I won't go in that crazy house," he said. "I'll go around to the back, the way I used to go in."

The back of the store was the place to find out how things were *really* run, Grandpa thought. All the freight was unloaded there. It was stored in the stock room, then it was sent to the different parts of the store to be sold.

There was an alley at the back of the store where horses and wagons used to back up to unload things: heavy cast-iron stoves and iron sinks, and all kinds of smaller things like washboards, flatirons, and lamp chimneys.

Grandpa walked through the crowds, pounding on the sidewalk with his gold-headed cane, although nobody could hear it. He came to the back alley.

Not one horse was in sight. Grandpa saw six huge trucks and trailers backed up to a platform.

The big iron doors were gone from the back of the store. There were no doors at all. Instead, half the wall was raised up, and Grandpa could see right inside. Men were unloading cartons from the trailers and onto hand trucks. They pushed the hand trucks to a conveyer belt inside the store, and unloaded the cartons again. The conveyer belt moved the cartons slowly up through a doorway to another floor. Grandpa went inside to get a closer look.

Things were moving pretty fast in there. Small electric tugs buzzed around, hooking onto dollies loaded high with cartons. These were labeled *Refrigerator* or *Hi-Fi Set,* or other things Grandpa had never heard of.

One tug came whizzing straight toward him. Grandpa jumped backwards to get out of the way. He landed right on the conveyer belt, and the belt carried him along with the cartons.

Up, up, and up Grandpa went, through the open doorway into another part of the store. He clung to the sides of the conveyer belt. He tried to sit up. A low beam overhead almost knocked his hat off.

As he was carried through the open doorway, Grandpa could see he was coming into an unpacking room. People were carrying cartons around and stacking them on tables. Other people were opening them up.

Grandpa didn't notice that he was coming

to the end of the conveyer belt. He went right off the end, heels over head, into a big canvas bin. Cartons began to pile in on top of him.

"Hey!" Grandpa shouted. "Stop that infernal thing!"

No one could hear him. The cartons kept coming. Pretty soon the bin was full and Grandpa was on the bottom.

The bin was on wheels. An electric tug slid up and hooked onto it. Grandpa felt himself being hauled away. When the bin stopped, Grandpa could hear somebody talking.

"Unpack these raincoats," a man said. "Then hang 'em up and steam out the wrinkles. Get price tags on them and hustle them upstairs for the sale. It looks like rain."

"I've got to get out of here," Grandpa muttered, "before I get steamed and price-tagged." He wiggled his way up through the cartons and climbed out of the bin.

Grandpa walked up and down the aisle of the unpacking room. Some women were sitting in front of stapling machines. They were stapling price tags on handkerchiefs and socks and skirts. Grandpa stamped his cane hard on the floor.

"Why aren't you all out in front selling things?" he shouted.

The women kept on with their work. No one even looked up.

"I'll make somebody hear me," Grandpa yelled. "I ran this store once and I'll do it again!"

Grandpa stamped around the unpacking room, looking for a stairway. Out of the corner of his eye he thought he saw a whole line of women in red dresses marching straight at him. He started to lift his hat to them, and then he saw they had no heads. It was just a long rack of dresses. A man behind the rack was pushing it.

Grandpa stepped quickly back into an open closet to get out of the way, but the dresses followed him in. The man who pushed the rack came in, and pushed a button on the wall of the closet. The closet door closed. Grandpa didn't know it, but he was in a freight elevator.

"Hey!" Grandpa yelled. "This closet's moving!"

He put his hand on top of his head. He thought the elevator was going to go right up through the roof. But it only went up one floor and stopped. The door opened.

The man pushed the rack of dresses out of the elevator and into a hall. Grandpa followed. It was a long hall with many turns in it. Other halls were coming in from the sides. On the walls were posters about the birthday sale. Each one had a picture of Grandpa at one end, and at the other, a picture of Bennett.

The hall was busy. People were coming and going. Some carried papers in their hands.

Some carried brief cases. They all seemed to be in a hurry.

"Hey!" Grandpa said. "You with the suit-case there!"

The man with the brief case paid no attention.

Grandpa rapped on the floor with his gold-headed cane. "Where can I find Bennett Follet?"

The man only looked at his wrist watch and hurried on up the hall.

A young woman came out of a door. She had some papers in her hand. She walked fast too. Grandpa hurried along beside her.

"Miss! Miss! Please listen!"

Grandpa pointed to his picture on a poster. "See! This is me! I'm Grandpa Follet!"

The young woman didn't answer. She opened a door and stepped inside. Grandpa followed her in.

Grandpa Follet found himself in a huge room full of machines. A young woman was sitting in front of each machine. The machines clattered and banged and whirred. Sometimes a bell would ring. The machines were writing letters. They were adding up columns of figures. They were punching holes in cards and stuffing them into envelopes to be mailed.

Grandpa looked at the young women sitting in front of the machines.

"What a lazy bunch!" he said. "You don't even have to lick the envelopes!"

Grandpa pulled his coattails in tight. He tried to slip down the aisle between the machines.

"Machines! Machines!" Grandpa growled, pulling his coat around him closer.

Every time a machine banged or thumped he tried to skip out of the way. He backed into a typewriter and a bell rang. He backed into a billing machine and it punched his coattails full of holes.

Grandpa tried to bellow over the clatter.

"Wait till I find that grandson of mine! I'll *feed* him to these machines!"

Then Grandpa found himself at the end of

the room, standing in front of a steel door.
Grandpa tried to open it to get away from the
machines. It was locked. He looked around to
see if the machines were chasing him.

Then suddenly Grandpa's nose wrinkled.
He sniffed.

"Money!" he said. "I could always smell money, and I'll bet you anything my grandson can smell money."

Grandpa's nose led him straight to the steel door. He thought he could hear jingling inside.

If Bennett is a true Follet, Grandpa thought, he'll be inside there counting up all the nickels and dimes and quarters.

Grandpa hammered on the door with his cane, but no one heard him.

A young man came up to the steel door. He was carrying two bags, one in each hand, and he walked as if the bags were very heavy. Grandpa stood to one side while the young man set the bags down, took a key out of his pocket, and opened the door. Then the young man reached down for the moneybags again. Grandpa slipped through the door ahead of him.

Inside, Grandpa heard the rattle and whir

of machines again. He followed the young man carrying the two moneybags. They passed more machines, with people sitting in front of them. Grandpa looked at the faces of the people. He couldn't see anybody anywhere that looked like a Follet.

The young man with the bags sat down in front of one of the machines. He turned one of the bags upside down into a tub on the top. A stream of coins clattered out. The young man pushed a button and the tub began to spin, rattle and bang. Pennies began to come out one spout at the bottom. Nickels came out another spout, and dimes out of another. The same thing happened to the half dollars and quarters.

Grandpa had never seen so much money. "And to think it all came from people who bought things right here in the store!" he said.

Rolls of coins were stacked on tables and piled on the floor. More coins were coming

out of the money separator as fast as the young man could dump another bag in.

"Hmmm," Grandpa said, "maybe there is some good in *some* machines." He remembered how he used to have to count up all the coins.

A young woman with a pencil and paper walked over to the money separator. She leaned over and read some figures that showed at the top, then she wrote the figures down.

"Here!" she said, handing a slip of paper to the young man who had carried the bags. "Send this money tally right down to Mr. Follet's office."

Grandpa listened carefully. "Office? Office! So that's where my grandson is!"

The young man at the money machine stood up.

"Hurry!" the young woman said. "Mr. Follet simply can't wait to get the money tally. He never leaves for lunch without it."

At last, Grandpa thought, I'm going to find my grandson. He started to follow the young man. Bennett's not very smart, but at least he's a Follet. A Follet ought to be able to talk to a Follet, even if one of 'em is a ghost and the other an idiot!

Grandpa thought the young man would leave the room and go down the hall, maybe up a staircase or two, to Bennett Follet's office. But he just walked over to one end of the same room where the money machines were.

"I don't understand this at all," Grandpa said.

Then, for the first time, Grandpa saw the suction tube system of the Follet Department Store. The people who worked in the store sent messages through the tube system. Sometimes they sent money. The suction tubes had been in the Follet Department Store a long, long time, but Grandpa had never seen them.

Grandpa looked up at the ceiling. There were dozens of large pipes, all coming down from above and ending at a large, flat desk where a young woman sat. The tube system looked something like a pipe organ without any keyboard.

The young man Grandpa was following

handed the money tally to the girl who sat in front of all the pipes. "Mr. Follet's waiting for this," he said. "Send it right down."

Grandpa watched closely. The girl at the table picked up a small brass cylinder the shape of a can, twisted the end off, put the paper with the money tally inside, and twisted the lid back on. Then she shoved the brass cylinder up into one of the tubes.

Grandpa bent down to look at the tubes more closely. He saw then that all of them were marked. This one was marked *Mr. Follet's Office.*

"Hmmm!" Grandpa said. "So my grandson is somewhere up this tube!" And he bent way over and peered up the suction tube as far as he could see.

That was a terrible mistake. A ghost isn't solid bulk like a human being. A ghost is flexible. A ghost is *too* flexible sometimes.

The suction caught Grandpa. He began to

stretch out like a wisp of smoke. First his head went into the tube, then the rest of him followed, and there was no way to stop.

Through the dark winding tube Grandpa went, twisting and turning between the walls of the Follet Department Store. Finally, he landed headfirst in a padded box on Bennett Follet's desk. The metal cylinder holding the money tally was lying in the box already. It had come through the suction tube just ahead of Grandpa.

Grandpa came out of the tube like a long, limp coil of rope. He'd been pulled out long and thin. He reached up his long, thin arms and pushed down on the top of his head until he squeezed himself back into his old shape again. He slipped down off the desk.

Grandpa noticed that the chair behind the

desk was empty. The polished desk had nothing on it — not a bottle of ink, not even a pen-wiper. The office floor had a deep, soft carpet. There was a deep, soft couch and deep, soft chairs.

And there, at last, was his grandson, standing beside the push-button panel with his back turned toward Grandpa. Bennett was pushing first one button, then another, making things happen all over the store.

"So there you are!" Grandpa said. "Up here in your fancy office, doing nothing but pushing little buttons!"

Bennett didn't answer. He was looking through the window at the crowds down on the main floor of the store.

Grandpa crossed the carpet and stood beside his grandson.

Bennett pushed another button. A phonograph record began to play through all the loudspeakers in the store:

"Happy birthday to you! Happy birthday to you. . . ."

"So you can't hear me, either!" Grandpa yelled. "Shut that thing off!"

Grandpa reached out with his gold-headed cane. He put the cane against the button. He pushed. The music stopped.

Bennett looked at the panel, surprised. He pushed the button again.

"Happy birthday, dear Follet Department Store, happy — "

Grandpa had pushed the button again.

"Now see here," Bennett said. "Who's fiddling with those push buttons?"

"I am," Grandpa yelled. "Look!"

He reached out with his cane and began pushing buttons as fast as he could: off buttons, on buttons, switches and lights.

The escalators in the Follet Department Store all stopped, started, stopped, and then ran backwards. The "up" elevators started going down and the "down" elevators started going up. Lights all over the store went off and on. "Happy Birthday" started playing again, with the bugle call blaring right in the middle of it.

Then Grandpa really did it. He stuck his

gold-headed cane in a little round socket where there was no light bulb.

Bennett Follet saw a big flash. Then he saw electric sparks and heard a hissing and crackling. Then he saw Grandpa, as Grandpa lit up like a light globe.

"Grandfather!" Bennett shouted. "You came back! You came back for the Big Birthday Sale!"

For a moment Grandpa glowed, frock coat, top hat, cane and all, as the electricity went through him. He shone brighter than any light globe in the Follet Department Store.

Then everything in the store went dark, including Grandpa. The lights went out. The adding machines wouldn't work. The elevators stopped between floors, and the escalators wouldn't move. In the basement, the conveyer belt stopped still with its load of cartons. The money separator stopped separating coins. The suction tubes didn't work.

Grandpa Follet looked through the window to the main floor below. The store with all the lights off looked gloomy. Everyone down there seemed to be standing still. The salesmen looked up at the dark light globes as if they didn't know what to do.

Then some children cried and some of the people began to leave. Grandpa saw them going through the glass front doors and into the bright daylight outside.

The Follet Department Store's giant birthday sale had come to a complete halt.

Grandpa leaned on his gold-headed cane. For the first time he felt like a useless old ghost. He felt longer and thinner than ever before. He felt as if the Follet Department Store was no place for him any more.

Bennett Follet picked up the telephone. That was still working anyway.

"Get the chief electrician," Bennett said. "Somebody **blew the main fuse**."

"Blew the main fuse!" Grandpa said. "Then I really *have* ruined the store!"

Bennett turned in the direction where he thought Grandpa was. It was just as if he heard Grandpa.

"Grandpa, you old rascal," he said. "It was you who pushed all the buttons. I believe you were trying to help. I think you wanted to run

the Follet Department Store, just like you used to."

"I ran it all right," Grandpa said. "Looks like I ran it right out of business."

Suddenly all the lights came on again.

"You see, Grandfather," Bennett said. "It just takes a minute to fix a fuse."

Bennett looked hard, trying to see Grandpa again, but he couldn't. Bennett hadn't been worried about the lights and elevators and things, because he had known what to do. But he *was* worried about Grandpa.

"You didn't do any real harm, Grandfather," he said. "You just haven't learned how to push buttons yet. See . . ."

Bennett pushed a button and the escalators started running. He pushed another and the elevators came down to the floors and let the people out.

Bennett couldn't see Grandpa, but he did see a button on the panel push in. He knew

Grandpa had pushed it. A little red light came on, and the "Happy Birthday" song played loud and cheery through the store.

"That's the way, Grandfather! That's the way to do it!" Bennett said. "Now you can push the buttons in the office, and I can stay down below with all the people and make them welcome!"

So now it's Grandpa Follet who pushes the buttons, and Bennett Follet who stands by the front door with his big friendly smile and greets the customers as they come in.

People don't know it, but Grandpa is the one who starts and stops the escalators, and turns the lights off and on and plays cheery music over the loudspeakers at holiday time.

If anybody did happen to be in the toy department of the Follet Department Store after closing hours, he would see electric trains start and stop. He would see all sorts of push-button toys working. Anybody would think they were doing it all by themselves, but not Bennett Follet. He's the only one who knows the Follet Department Store is really run by old Grandpa Follet himself, with just nothing but push buttons.